Grayso e

A Fox River tale about baseball, bones... and what matters most.

Written by Harold William Thorpe
Illustrated by Aaron Boyd

LITTLE CREEK PRESS
A DIVISION OF KRISTIN MITCHELL DESIGN, LLC

Mineral Point, Wisconsin USA

Published by Little Creek Press®
A Division of Kristin Mitchell Design, LLC
5341 Sunny Ridge Road
Mineral Point, Wisconsin 53565

Illustrator: Aaron Boyd
Editor: Tiffany Francois
Book Design and Project Coordination:
Little Creek Press

Limited First Edition
November 2014

Printed in Wisconsin, United States of America.

For more information or to order books:
www.littlecreekpress.com

Library of Congress Control Number: 2014954143

ISBN-10: 0989978451
ISBN-13: 978-0-9899784-5-3

Grayson's Garage is dedicated to my loquacious grandson, Grayson Thorpe, who, I believe, could talk our hungry dog out of her evening meal. If I'd have allowed Grayson, in the book, to have negotiated with the State Historical Society, there would have been less waiting and my story would have been much shorter.

Acknowledgements

I thank Grayson's grandmother Marilyn Hein for her editorial suggestions during the refinement of *Grayson's Garage*. I also thank my publisher, Kristin Mitchell, her Little Creek Press staff, and her editor Tiffany Francois for their guidance throughout the book's development.

Table of Contents

The Championship Ballgame 7

Grayson's Friend Alex 13

Challenging KAOS 17

Grayson's Garage Will Be Delayed 21

Money to Fix Alex's Foot 27

Grayson May Never Get His Garage 31

Grayson Hates Waiting 37

Grayson and Alex Meet Sergeant Digby 43

The Best Digging Crew in Butte des Morts 49

Grayson Finds Treasure 53

Grayson's Dilemma 57

Will Alex Live? 63

Another Championship Game 69

The Championship Ballgame

Grayson Thorpe eyed the pitcher as he prepared to throw the ball. The game was on the line. His Butte des Morts (pronounced Bu-da-more) Lion's team had two outs in the last inning and they were one run behind. Each time at bat, Grayson had hit the ball hard but right at a fielder.

The pitcher threw the ball. The umpire called, "Strike one."

Grayson looked to first base where his best friend, Alex, stood near the bag. Grayson knew that Alex would need a running start to have a chance to score so he motioned for Alex to take a bigger lead, but Alex didn't notice.

The pitcher threw the ball fast, and Grayson swung and missed. He wanted to hit the ball hard because he knew it would take a long drive to get Alex home.

The pitcher looked confident. One more pitch and he'd win the game. Grayson wiggled his feet, looked toward Coach Meyer in the dugout, and then eyed the pitcher.

The ball flew toward him, and Grayson started to swing, but he held back.

"Ball one," the umpire called.

Grayson backed away from the plate and looked toward Alex at first. He didn't think his friend had enough lead off the base.

But Alex didn't look in his direction. He stared toward second base, ready to run at the sound of the bat hitting the ball.

Grayson swung the bat twice, hitched up his pants, and stepped back into the batter's box. The pitcher raised the ball to his chest. Grayson leaned back, waiting for the pitch.

He expected a fast ball—knew the pitcher would try to throw it past him. He set his feet and waited. The ball came down the middle of the plate. Grayson swung hard and made solid contact. As he rounded first base he could see the outfielder chasing the ball toward the fence. He looked toward second base and saw Alex step on the bag, but Grayson was catching up fast. By the time Alex touched third base, Grayson was running at his heels, and they ran toward home plate together. But Grayson had to slow to not run over his friend. He looked back and saw the shortstop with the ball, ready to throw it to the catcher who stood on home plate.

Grayson hollered, "Run, Alex. Run fast."

They'd win the game if they both scored. And they were ten feet from home plate when, out of the corner of his eye, Grayson saw the ball flying at the catcher. He reached forward to his friend who was running his fastest, but as Alex stepped toward home plate, he stumbled and fell face-first into the base path, two feet short of the plate.

Grayson tripped over Alex and flew into the dirt.

The catcher grabbed the ball and tagged them both.

Harold William Thorpe

The umpire shouted, "You're out!"

Alex sat on the base path, eyeing his twisted foot, tears streaking his dirt covered face.

At first Grayson wanted to scream at Alex. But when he looked at his heartbroken friend, he felt miserable. Even with his twisted foot, Alex tried his hardest and did his best.

Their baseball season was over until next summer.

February days in Wisconsin were cold, so Alex and Grayson often played in his cousins' heated garage. Wyatt, Grayson's older cousin, pushed his scooter around in circles, and Grayson and Alex ran behind, waiting their turn. But Alex tripped as he tried to keep up. Grayson wished that Alex could run and play like his other friends. It made him sad to see Alex stumble across the garage floor. He hoped the doctors could find a way to fix his best friend's twisted foot.

When it was Alex's turn to ride the scooter, he had trouble getting started. His turned-in right foot slipped off the scooter.

"Put your left foot up," Wyatt said. "Try pushing with your right."

But when Alex tried it that way, the back wheels ran over his toes. He dropped to the floor and rubbed his foot. "I'll just watch."

Alex sat on the hard cement steps and smiled toward his friends. Grayson knew that Alex sat and watched lots of times, and he wished that he could help somehow. Grayson thought he'd cry if he had to sit and watch his friends play, but Alex always had a smile on his face.

And because he didn't know how he could help, Grayson took Alex's turn on the scooter.

More than anything, Grayson wanted a heated garage like his cousins' garage. All winter, Wyatt and his sister, Aubrey, played in it. They hit wiffle balls. They rode Wyatt's tractor. They pushed the scooter in circles. They tossed Frisbees. And Wyatt helped his father wash their car in that garage. But best of all, they could do these things all winter when, outside, the snow piled high and the cold air froze their fingers.

Grayson's Friend Alex

Grayson and Alex walked from the bus. The school year was almost over and his classmates were excited. All of them talked about tomorrow's spring track meet. Grayson, a third grader, thought he could run fast, but not as fast as some of the fourth grade students that he'd compete against, so he decided to run the four hundred meter race this year. Alex said he'd run the one hundred meter dash.

"You can never beat those fourth graders in the one hundred meters," Grayson said.

"I may not beat all the third graders either. I didn't beat anyone last year. But I'm not going to run last place this year." Alex smiled as he stumbled forward to keep up with Grayson. "I've been practicing. And I'll do better. I just know it."

Grayson liked his friend's cheeriness. No matter how hard the task, Alex always tried his best. And he always expected to do better. Grayson wasn't so confident that Alex could run fast enough, but he wouldn't tell his friend that. Alex was really good at most things. He just couldn't run fast. Grayson didn't know why he kept trying.

After school the next day, Grayson and Alex warmed up for their races. Their physical education teacher had told them how important warming up was, especially on these cool days. So they jogged side by side up and down the infield grass. Then they lay on their backs and stretched their leg muscles.

"Are you sure that you want to run the one hundred meter race?" Grayson said. "You'd have a better chance in a longer one."

"After last year's race, I told myself that I'll do better next year, that I'd not run in last place. And I won't."

Grayson hoped that his friend was right.

They ran the longer races first, and when the four hundred meter race was called, Grayson took off his jacket and turned toward the track. Alex ran along with him to the start line and, as Grayson stood waiting for the starter's signal, Alex shouted, "I'll be cheering for you."

Grayson smiled. It felt good to have Alex for a friend.

And Grayson felt good after his race was over. He didn't win a ribbon, but he came close.

While Grayson stood waiting for the signal to start the one hundred meter dash, he flashed a thumbs-up sign to his friend at the start line. Alex looked at him for a moment, but he didn't smile. Then he turned his head and stared down the track toward the finish line.

Grayson could see that Alex was determined. He always tried his hardest.

Their physical education teacher hollered, "Go!"

Alex got a good start, but he stumbled part way down the track and, by the end of the race, all the other runners had streaked past him.

Grayson felt miserable for his friend. He'd run in last place again this year.

That night at the dinner table when Grayson told his parents about the races, he thought about the sad look on his friend's face. "I wish they could fix Alex's foot."

"The doctors tried therapy and a cast," Grayson's father said, "but they didn't help."

"There must be something they can do."

"Surgery, but his parents can't afford it."

"I'll give them my birthday money," Grayson said. "I was saving for a Skylander, but I don't have enough money to buy the Skylander Giant set, anyhow."

"That's sweet of you, my dear," his mother said. "But it's not nearly enough."

"Dad?" When his father didn't answer, Grayson could see that he was thinking.

"Dad?"

His father looked up. "I was wondering if the Butte des Morts Lion's Club would help."

"They have fundraisers to help the community," Grayson's mother said.

"I think I'll talk to Mr. Ehlert," Grayson's father said.

"Do you think they can help Alex?"

"Maybe they will. I'll ask."

"Grayson," his mother said, "there's something else we'd like to tell you."

"Oh."

"It's good news," his father said. "We've decided to build a house. We bought a lot, just around the corner."

"Can we have a heated garage?"

Challenging KAOS

Grayson attached his transporter to the TV set, took Spyro, Trigger Happy, and Gill Grunt from their case, and set the figures out on the coffee table. Grayson's cousin Wyatt had received a Skylander Giant system for a Christmas present, and he had given his starter set to Grayson. Alex said that he didn't have any TV games and that he'd never played Skylander before. He'd be here in a few minutes and Grayson wanted to be ready to show him the game. He knew that Alex would learn fast. He was one of the best students in their class.

"KAOS is trying to destroy Skyland," Grayson said, "and we've got to stop him. But first we'll have to fight his Arkeyan minions."

"How do we do that?"

Grayson pointed to the three figures on the coffee table. "This one is named Spyro, this one Trigger Happy, and this is Gill Grunt. You take your pick, I'll choose one, and, together, we'll fight his minions."

Alex paused for a moment. Then he pointed to Spyro. "What do I do?"

"You place him in the portal of power." Grayson pointed to the container in front of his TV set. "I'll select." He hesitated. "Let's see." Then he grabbed Gil Grunt and set him in the portal. "You put Spyro in here and then watch the TV screen."

Two magnificent figures appeared in full armament on the screen. Grayson showed Alex how to use the controls. "We'll get in our robot and go look for KAOS's minion."

"What do we do when we find him?"

"I'll throw light gears at him and you throw punches. If we hit him enough we can drive his health bar down to zero."

"What does that do?"

"When we've taken his health away, then he's done for. But KAOS will be hard to beat."

When they found the minion, Grayson threw volleys of light gears toward him, and then he stopped and said, "Okay, Alex, start punching him."

Alex threw punches non-stop, and soon the minion's health bar was driven to the bottom of the gauge.

"You're good, Alex," Grayson said. "We'll take down his other minion, and then we'll go after KAOS."

"This is easy. My robot's legs are strong."

But defeating KAOS wasn't so easy. Grayson threw light gears and Alex threw lots of punches, but they couldn't bring him down.

Grayson's mother brought glasses of orange juice and a plate of pumpkin bread. "You boys must be thirsty. You fought hard. I thought the living room was coming down."

Harold William Thorpe

"Mom, will you buy me Skylander Giant for my birthday? It has big, really tough fighters. Thumpback can beat anyone."

His mother frowned at him. "Never satisfied, now are you? You've only had this set a month."

"But it's too easy." Grayson knew that was a fib. He still hadn't taken down KAOS.

"With building the house, we won't have the money this year. Are there inexpensive figures we can buy for this set?"

"Yes, Mother."

"Does Skylander Giant cost a lot?" Alex said.

"It sure does. It'd cost almost five hundred dollars to buy everything." Grayson buttered a slice of pumpkin bread and took a bite. "I'd never be able to save enough for it." He thought about Jim Hawkins in *Treasure Island,* the story his teacher had given him to read. "Maybe we could search for a pirate's treasure."

Grayson didn't continue to pester his mother. He wanted Skylander Giant, but he wanted his garage even more.

Grayson's Garage Will Be Delayed

Grayson dug in the dirt pile with his little shovel while he watched his father maneuver the backhoe and scoop dirt from the hole he was digging for the house's foundation. Grayson wondered where the garage would be. It didn't seem there was a place for that. When his father stopped for lunch, Grayson said, "It doesn't look big enough for a garage. Where will that be?"

"Mother and I decided to build the house a bit larger than we'd planned at first, so we'll spend the money on the house this year."

"We won't have a garage?"

"We'll have one later, after the house is done."

Any garage would be okay, Grayson thought, even if it wasn't heated. "We have to build a garage."

"Maybe next year."

Grayson threw down his shovel, turned away from the hole, and walked toward the street. His father jumped from the machine and hollered, "Hey, it's lunch time. Let's go home to eat."

But Grayson wasn't hungry. He kept walking. All he could think about was that garage that he wouldn't have. When his parents had said they'd build a new house, he was excited. He'd gone to his room, took his pad from a drawer, and began to write a list of the things he could play in the garage. He thought about it in school, and, when he had a new idea, he'd rush home and add it to his list. He tried to think of things that Wyatt didn't have in his garage. He wrote, "*a dart board, a fussball table.*"

He didn't know how to spell foosball, and he didn't think it would fit in their new garage if they kept their cars inside, but he liked the idea anyway. Wyatt didn't have one. And he wrote down *table tennis*, too, but he was sure that wouldn't fit.

His mother and dad knew how much he wanted that garage. He didn't count at all in their plans. They didn't care about him. Even though his dad had told him not to throw rocks, he picked one up and threw it as far as he could. He didn't care, either.

That night at the dinner table, his mother said, "You must be hungry. You didn't come home for lunch."

"Not really."

"I made your favorite cheesy breadsticks."

Grayson picked at his food.

"I know you're unhappy because we won't have a garage right away," his father said.

"Grayson," his mother said, "eat your meal. You haven't eaten anything since breakfast."

Grayson cut a small piece of cheesy breadstick but didn't put it in his mouth.

"You're old enough to know that once we've built the foundation, we can't make it bigger," his father said. "But we can always add a garage. And we will."

His mother bent over and gave him a kiss. "This way, you'll have a bigger room to play in with your friends. And you can decide how to decorate it."

Grayson frowned. "I already have a room. I don't need a new house for that."

"We think you'll really like the bigger room."

"I can't hit wiffle balls in my room." He looked toward his dad. "And I can't play table tennis."

Grayson's father didn't say anything, but Grayson could tell by the look on his dad's face that he wouldn't have table tennis in the garage. Grayson knew that already.

School was out and each day the house progressed a little more toward completion. Even though he was still irritated and sad about not having a garage yet, he enjoyed watching his father build their house. At first, it had just been a slab of cement and boards around the edge reaching toward the sky. Then the rooms started to take shape, and Grayson's father took him inside and showed him where his bedroom would be. He pointed toward one wall. "That will probably be a good place for your bed, but where would you like it?"

It didn't look much like a room yet, just a bunch of sticks, so Grayson wasn't sure. "Can I have a TV set in here?"

"We'll have to talk about that. I don't think your mother—" His dad pointed toward the corner. "There'll be a closet here. Big enough for your clothes and all your toys." Before Grayson had time to think about his big closet, his father pointed to the far wall. "Over there, the window will be so big, and we're so high up, that you'll be able to see all the way to the lake."

Grayson could see that his father was more excited about his new, big bedroom than he felt. And he didn't have a TV in his room now, even though he'd begged for one, so he supposed that his mother wouldn't be too keen on having one in his new room. It wasn't fair that he'd not get his garage.

But when his mother told him the news at dinner, he forgot how unhappy he was about the garage.

"I talked with Mr. Ehlert today. He said the Lion's Club, at their next meeting, will discuss a fundraiser for Alex's operation."

Grayson was excited when he went to bed that night. He couldn't wait until the next day when he'd see Alex.

Money to Fix
Alex's Foot

Once the outside walls were up and sided, the men arrived to enclose the roof.

Alex and Grayson sat on the dirt pile and watched the men scramble across the rafters while they spread sheeting and nailed shingles to the plywood.

"I wouldn't want to work up that high," Grayson said.

"Maybe I would after the doctors fix my foot. Do you think the Lion's Club will be able to get the money?"

"Dad said it might take awhile, but they're going to have raffles at the August Carp Fest, and the ladies will have bake sales all summer long."

Grayson knew that lots of people came to Butte des Morts each August when it held its annual festival. He thought to call it Carp Fest was strange because that was a large fish that few people wanted. But his dad said the name caught their attention and attracted people.

Grayson tossed a rock down the dirt pile and watched it roll into the grass. "Mother says she's going to ask all the ladies in town to donate things for a big rummage sale." He tossed another stone toward the bigger one at the bottom.

"Dad says we'll need thousands of dollars."

"Winneconne has garage sales all over town once a year. And they make lots of money. Our baseball coach made over a hundred dollars last year. Maybe we can, too."

"It'll take lots of garage sales."

"I'll donate all my old toys."

"Will you let me choose some first?"

Grayson knew that Alex didn't have many toys. "Oh, sure. You can take your pick."

"Are you going to sell your baseball glove?"

"Not my new one." Alex's glove was ripped and way too small. "But you can have my old one. It's still pretty good."

"Do you have something to help me run faster?"

Grayson thought back to the final game last summer. "You hit the ball really good. And you throw good, too."

"Do you think they'll get my foot fixed this summer?" Alex looked at Grayson's long straight legs. "I'm praying for straight legs."

"You'll need to pray harder now that the finish line is close. I'll say a prayer tonight, too."

"Will they ever get enough money? I hope it's soon."

"Dad says I'll have to wait until next year for my garage. We'll both have to wait, I think." Grayson picked up a stone and threw it hard against the pine tree. "I hate waiting."

Alex smiled broadly. "It's not so bad when there's something good to wait for."

Grayson didn't know how Alex could stay so cheerful. He didn't feel like smiling. He looked at Alex's bent foot. But he only had a garage to wait for.

The windows and doors had been installed, the interior dry-walled, the wood floors laid, and the trim and cabinetry put in. Grayson's mother said they'd be in their new house by Labor Day. Grayson was excited, but he still wanted a garage.

Summer was almost over. He'd be back in school soon after they moved into their new house. His baseball team hadn't won many games, but he knew they'd be better next year when most of his teammates would be a year older. He hoped that Alex's foot would be fixed by then. And he expected to have a garage to play in next year. His father had said they'd dig its foundation in spring.

Grayson May Never Get His Garage

Grayson watched his father unload the skid steer from the trailer. He was excited. He'd soon have his garage. Today his father would skim the sod and topsoil and pile it near the back of the yard. He'd use it later when he put in the lawn. Alex and Grayson looked down from the dirt pile. They watched the machine lurch this way and that as it scooped the earth and piled it high.

"It must be fun to drive the skid steer," Alex said. "Your dad controls it mostly with his hands."

"He lets me drive it sometimes."

"You drive it alone?"

Grayson started to say yes, but he knew that wasn't true. "I steer it and move the levers, but Dad won't let me drive it alone."

"You dig dirt with it?"

Grayson wished that he could, but his dad had said, "Someday, but not yet."

"I drive it across the yard. But it's more fun than driving Wyatt's tractor."

"Do you think the Lion's Club will earn enough money before summer is over?"

"Mom says they've earned a lot, that maybe they'll have enough money by Thanksgiving or Christmas."

"That seems like a long time." Alex smiled. "I guess you'll have your new garage first."

Grayson hoped so. But he didn't want to say it. "Maybe someone will donate lots of money, and we can both celebrate."

"Yeah, we can have a big I-Got-My-Wish party."

"We'll have it together." But Grayson didn't think there'd be near enough money for Alex's operation by the time his garage was ready.

They watched Grayson's dad pile his last load high, clean out the scoop, and drive the skid steer back onto his trailer.

"What now?" Alex said.

"Come back tomorrow, early. He'll rent a back-hoe and dig the hole. He said that he wants to begin digging by eight o'clock."

"Will he get it done tomorrow?"

"He'd better. The men are coming to lay the footings for the garage the next day."

"I'll be here early."

Grayson was so excited that he ran outside the next morning before eating. His mother hauled him back into the house. "Oh, no. Not without breakfast, young man."

Alex knocked on his door before Grayson had finished eating and before Grayson's father had returned with the back-hoe.

Grayson supposed that Alex got away without taking time to eat. But he didn't dare say anything for fear his mother would slow them further by sitting his friend down at the table.

They were high on a dirt pile when Grayson's dad pulled the trailer and back-hoe into the drive.

Grayson let out his breath and grabbed Alex's arm when the big shovel lowered to the ground. The bucket unfolded and extended to its farthest reach, faltered for a moment, and then stuttered as it cut through the thick clay soil. "This is it. I'll soon have my garage."

Then he thought about Alex's operation. Would he soon have that?

Grayson's father swung the cab and shovel around, and he dumped the load on the nearest dirt pile. He swung the arm and bucket back over the hole, lowered the scoop again, and then lifted and dumped another load. The boys watched him do this three more times.

"The hole's getting big," Alex said.

Grayson wanted to slide down the dirt pile and look into the excavation, but his father had warned them, "Stay up there or I'll send you in the house. I can't be worrying about two boys underfoot."

And Grayson knew he would, too. But he so wanted to look down into that hole.

Then his father stopped, turned the engine off, and hopped down from the cab.

Grayson hollered, "What's wrong, Dad?"

He started to slide down the dirt pile, but his father held up a hand and shook his head no.

Grayson climbed back up next to Alex. His father jumped into the hole. All Grayson could see was his back as he bent over. "What is it?" He got no answer. He could see his father intently fingering through some debris. "Dad! What's wrong?"

His father straightened and beckoned the boys down. In a moment they were looking into the hole. "What is it, Dad?"

His father held up an old bone.

"A dog buried that?" Alex said.

"No, it wasn't a dog. It's much too deep for that."

It was a long bone, longer than any Grayson had seen his neighbor's dog gnawing on.

"Mr. Kontos said there used to be lots of deer here. They'd come down to the lake to drink."

Mr. Kontos had lived in Butte des Morts since he was a boy and knew more about the area and its history than anyone. Many years before, his father had started Butte des Morts' famous White House Inn, and Mr. Kontos and other investors had dug channels from the lake, sold building lots, and doubled the size of the community.

"I don't think it's a bone from a deer," Grayson's father said.

"Then what is it?"

"I'm not sure, but I think we'd better call the State Historical Society."

"The Historical Society?" He'd learned about them. His teacher had written to get information about Winneconne's history. "Why the Historical Society?"

"They'll know what we should do."

Grayson began to feel worried, and he was afraid to hear the answer to his next question. "Will we have to stop digging?"

"I don't know, son." His father climbed out of the hole and faced Grayson. "This may be a very old bone. We may have dug into an ancient Indian burial ground."

Grayson felt terrible. Mr. Kontos had told him that Indians had once been buried here—that Butte des Morts was a French name—and it meant Hill of the Dead.

"Can't we just keep digging and throw these bones into the bottom of the hole?"

Grayson's dad gave him a look that Grayson had seen before. And it meant for him to use his head. But Grayson didn't want to use his head, not now, not after waiting for so long. He wanted a garage.

Grayson Hates Waiting

Grayson and his Grandpa Thorpe spent lots of time together talking about history. Grayson loved to hear Grandpa tell what life had been like in Butte des Morts. Grandpa said that three hundred years ago, and even long before, Indian tribes came to the Fox River area to harvest wild rice from the marshes. Whether from natural death or death in battle, many Indians took their last breath on the hill overlooking the river. The bones of the dead, covered with dirt after each burial, piled high. French missionaries, trappers, and voyagers began to call one hill Grand (big) Butte des Morts and another hill that was further down river but north of Lake Winnebago, Petit (little) Butte des Morts.

In 1818 Augustin Grignon (pronounced Green-yo) established a trading post above the river and sold goods to the many pioneers who traveled up the Fox River toward the Wisconsin River, the Mississippi River, the Missouri River, and the riches and dangers of far western lands. Years later the state built a dam on the Fox River at Neenah, and this caused the river below the trading post to widen into a large but shallow body of water, Lake Butte des Morts.

And it was in the village of Butte des Morts, an unincorporated community of one thousand residents, that Grayson's father dug the hole in which he'd lay the footings for his new garage.

But the state had rules when old bones were uncovered. And those rules said they must get permission before another shovel of dirt could be taken from the hole.

Grayson didn't much like rules at home or school, but he especially disliked these that delayed building the garage that he'd wished for so long.

"How long will we have to wait?"

"I called the Wisconsin Historical Society and they said I must contact the burial sites preservation program. And someone there will determine if they might be old human bones."

"But how long will that take?"

"I don't know, Grayson. We'll just have to wait."

But Grayson hated waiting.

A week passed and they'd heard nothing.

"Dad, when will they come?"

"I don't know, son."

Another week passed and Grayson began to think he'd never get his garage. He liked his new room, lots, but he'd trade it for a garage.

"Dad, can't you do something?"

"It's been more than two weeks," Grayson's mother said. "Maybe you should contact them again."

Grayson paced the floor while his dad talked on the telephone. He hoped his father could start digging again.

And when his father lowered and folded his cell phone, Grayson grabbed his arm. "Can you dig now?"

"I'm afraid not, son." His father placed the phone back in his pocket. "The law says they must follow a procedure."

"What's that?"

"The burial sites preservation program is understaffed, but they said I can call the sheriff's office and they'll get someone here as soon as he's available."

"Then do it," Grayson's mother said. "Maybe he can get things moving."

Days passed and no word came. While Grayson waited he played ball games, he fought KAOS, and he played with Alex. Still, no word came. The Lion's Club was raising money so fast that Grayson began to think Alex would get his foot fixed before he'd get his garage. His mother said that he shouldn't compare the two, but he was beginning to feel jealous. And he continued to press his dad for news.

"Have you heard from the sheriff, Dad?"

"He's terribly busy and understaffed, too. He hasn't found anyone who can do it."

"How long will it take after they contact the man?"

"It depends on what they find. We might have to get a permit from the Historical Society to proceed."

"How long will that take?"

"Even longer if they believe they're old tribal bones. They may tell us to hire an archeologist to help move the bones properly."

"Can't we ask our neighbors to turn their dogs loose for a few nights?"

"Grayson!" His mother looked stern. "How would you like for someone to dig up your great-grandfather's bones?"

Grayson knew his mother was right. But he wished that he didn't live in Butte des Morts.

Harold William Thorpe

Grayson and Alex Meet Sergeant Digby

Grayson and Alex sat alongside the garage hole, no bigger now than the day his father had started scooping out dirt with the back-hoe.

"I never thought that an old bone would keep me from having a garage."

"Mother tells me to be patient," Alex said.

"My cousin Aubrey says that patience is an excuse. If it's worth doing, it's worth doing now."

"Aubrey doesn't need money to fix her foot."

"Aubrey could do cartwheels with a broken leg. It'd take more than a broken leg to slow her down."

Grayson saw movement on the lawn near where his father had stopped digging. He looked closer and saw a strange little figure emerge from a hole. He grabbed Alex's shoulder. "Look over there." He pointed. "It's a gopher." He stared and shook cobwebs from his brain. The WWII history Grandpa Thorpe talked about came alive in his head. He could hardly believe what he saw. "Isn't he wearing clothes?"

And he was. It was an odd looking gopher, indeed. He wore khaki trousers, a tan shirt, and an olive color trench coat that had red, v-shaped stripes on the chest and sleeves.

But when Grayson stood to look closer, the gopher didn't run away. Instead, he came nearer. And when he stood in front of Grayson, he saluted. "Sergeant Digby O'Reilly reporting for duty, Sir."

"Sir?"

"We're prim 'n' proper in the British army—Sir! Even when you're outa uniform."

"I don't see any army?"

"Right, Sir! We've had fam in the British Expeditionary Force right up to the Big War. My Great-Great-Great Grandfather fought at Dunkirk."

Grayson wasn't sure, but he thought the Big War might have been fought when his grandfather was a boy.

"But what are you doing here?"

"My pappy stole away on a ship from London. He got into a food container and stayed in the nosebag all the way to Green Bay. He met my mother there."

"In the nosebag?"

"He ate his way here, old chap—" Sergeant Digby had slumped a bit during their conversation, but he snapped to attention. "Sir!"

"I've never been called sir."

Harold William Thorpe

"You've spent so much time lookin' into this hole that I supposed you're top banana in these diggins. And that makes you General." He pointed to Alex. "He's your adjutant?"

"My—?"

"Don't be daft, General—Sir!"

Grayson could see that Sergeant Digby was annoyed.

"Your assistant." Digby frowned so sternly that his glasses dropped to the end of his nose. And they would have fallen off if his thick whiskers hadn't rescued them. "Most generals I've known need lots of help."

Grayson looked toward his friend. "Hear that, adjutant." They laughed together.

"But I don't see an army."

"They're off on a bimble. Should be back soon."

"A what?"

"They're doing scouting. Can't be too careful. Never know when a nasty bloke's flying around."

"I don't know anyone nasty, not in Butte des Morts."

"Octavious and Mac come around at night. But we're in our jimjams by then."

"Octavious? Jimjams?"

"You call them jammies. And Octavious and Mac are two owls who live in the big evergreen tree down Maple Street. But they mostly fly to the Trading Post looking for Harry."

"I know everyone in Butte des Morts, but I don't know Harry."

"Harry Mouse. He's an addled bloke, but he's cool beans, alright. Those knob heads think they'll filch his cheese, but they don't know diddly squat. One of these days Harry'll throw a wobbler and pepper their behinds. And that'll be ticketyboo with me."

Grayson had no idea what Sergeant Digby had just said. But Grayson didn't speak British English, so he supposed that he'd have to look in this book's glossary for an explanation.

"Let's get down to brass tacks, Sir!" Sergeant Digby said. "What do you have in mind for our duty?"

"What can you do?"

"Why, Sir, we're the best diggin' brigade in Butte des Morts."

The Best Digging Crew
in Butte des Morts

Grayson and Alex returned the next morning to meet Sergeant Digby and his men. He had no idea what the sergeant could do to help, but he'd said they were the best, so maybe they could help dig the garage hole. But he didn't tell his dad about this digging crew.

The sergeant had already gathered his men, and the brigade stood at ease when the boys arrived. As soon as Sergeant Digby saw Grayson, he shouted his command: "Tention!" and a back yard full of gophers stood erect and shouldered their shovels.

"Awaiting your orders, Sir!"

Grayson turned to Alex. "What can we have them do?"

"Maybe they've seen more bones down there."

"Sergeant Digby," Grayson called to him. "Do your men know if the hole is full of bones?"

The sergeant called toward his brigade, "At ease, men." Then he motioned to one of his troopers. "You, Ducky, up here."

A short, thin, and scruffy looking gopher waddled to the front. Grayson thought he looked even stranger than the sergeant. He wore the usual army khaki uniform, but it was torn and tattered. He wore a miner's hat with a gaslight on the top, carried a pickaxe instead of a shovel, and had firecrackers stuffed in all his pockets.

"Ducky's my demolition man," Sergeant Digby explained.

"Demolition?"

"Yes, Sir! If the going gets rough, we send him into the hole to set charges and blow though the debris. Sometimes he doesn't get out in time." Sergeant Digby turned back to his man. "Ducky, have you seen any old bones down in the holes?"

"Not on your Nelly, sir. We stay away from bones. The dogs, you know."

The sergeant turned back to Grayson. "My men don't like to rile your neighborhood dogs. They go bonkers if they think we're after their bones."

Ducky dug in his pocket and pulled out a small gold ring. "I thought this looked kinda pretty, so I snatched it on our last dig. We find lots of bits and bobs underground."

Grayson and Alex slid down the dirt pile together. "Is that real gold?" Grayson said. "May I see it?" He held out his hand. Then he remembered his manners. "Please?"

Grayson brushed dirt off the ring, looked closely, and then handed it to Alex. "Do you think this is gold?"

Alex turned the ring in his fingers. "Maybe it's pirate treasure."

"Where did you find this?" Grayson asked Ducky.

"Here and there. Never know what thingy you'll run into when you're diggin'."

Harold William Thorpe

"Is it pirate's treasure?" Grayson said.

"Hain't seen no pirates," Ducky said. "Not underground, anyways. But there's a pile of things in the other corner of your yard."

"What kind of things?" Grayson said.

"Lots of thingys, but mostly old bottles."

"I've read that old bottles can be worth lots of money," Alex said.

Grayson thought about the Skylander Giant set that he wanted. That cost lots of money.

He turned to Sergeant Digby. "You wanted orders? Have your men dig for those—those thingys they saw across the yard."

"Yes, Sir!" Sergeant Digby saluted smartly, turned on his heel, and shouted toward his brigade, "Shoulder those shovels, men. Spread out and start diggin'. Report back what you find."

Grayson had never seen such a flurry of activity. A yard full of gophers raced across the grass to the far corner, then threw dirt in every direction. And soon they'd all disappeared underground. He sure hoped they'd come back with a pirate's treasure, or something he could sell to buy those giant Skylanders.

Grayson Finds Treasure

Digby's brigade worked through the day while Grayson watched from the dirt pile. Early afternoon, Ducky reported that they'd found bits and bobs in the back corner of Grayson's yard. But the going was rough, and his small explosives weren't blasting through into the treasure-trove.

Sergeant Digby called up to Grayson. "We need to put some elbow grease into it, old chap. Would you mind giving us a hand?"

Grayson was excited when he heard they were close to the treasure, so he took his little shovel from his father's shed and went to help Digby's brigade. The gophers had dug and blasted so many holes that digging through them was easy, so Grayson dug fast.

"Eye up, lad. Wouldn't want to put the kibosh on the whole shebang by breaking the thingys."

So Grayson slowed, but he made good progress, and by mid-afternoon he was finding a few broken bottles. Then his shovel hit a larger piece. He stooped down and gently peeled dirt away with his fingers. Ducky worked from the other side, but when he took out a firecracker and shoved it alongside the bottle, Sergeant Digby hollered, "Don't be a dipstick, my man. You break that thingy and I'll give you the old heave ho. Go take a kip."

Digby pushed Ducky aside, and worked alongside Grayson. "It's been a long day. He's clapped out." The sergeant scrapped dirt away and the bottle loosened. "That old chap knows his onions. Not like him to raddle like that."

They eased the bottle from the hole. Grayson turned it in his hands while he dusted it off. "It's not very big."

The sergeant eyed the bottle when Grayson held it toward him. "A strange one, though. There's some writing on it."

The bottle was round with a short neck, and it had writing along the side. Grayson read each letter aloud—"M,A,N,H,A,T,T,A,N. It says, Man—hat—tan on its side."

"That's sound, old chap. Could be worth a wad."

Grayson wondered if it might be worth enough to buy the whole Skylander Giant set.

They continued to find jars as they dug, but none quite as interesting as that first one. They all looked old, though, and Grayson remembered Alex telling him that old jars can be worth lots of money.

Grayson's Dilemma

Grayson's father read the letter from the sheriff's office and then handed it to his mother.

"What does it say?" Grayson asked.

"They can't get out here to inspect our site until their volunteers return for university classes in late summer."

"We'll have to wait until after school begins to start our garage?"

"Maybe longer."

Grayson left the house in a bad mood. He was beginning to think that he may never get his garage. He walked to the small playground that the Butte des Morts Lion's Club had installed in the center of town and sat on a swing seat. He didn't feel like talking, so he was glad that none of his friends were there.

He looked across the street to the old Trading Post, the biggest building in town. He'd heard that it was also the oldest building in the county.

Mr. Kontos said that it had been there for almost two hundred years. And Grayson supposed that it had. Mr. Kontos knew more about Butte des Morts history than anyone in town.

Grayson wondered if any of the bottles he'd found were as old as that building. His father had boxed them and sent them to a collector he knew in Madison. Maybe they'd bring enough money to buy a Skylander Giant set. His father had promised that the money would be his. He began to feel better as he thought about the game. He wanted to play with the big Skylanders—Thumpback, Eye Brawl, and Ninjini. For sure, he'd take down KAOS and save Skyland if he had them.

"Grayson," Alex called as he walked toward the playground. "Have you heard about the bottles, yet?"

"Not yet." Grayson was about to say they'd heard from the sheriff's office, but decided he didn't want to talk about the garage. "Do you think we can beat Winneconne this Saturday?"

Their Lion's team had only won three games all summer, so Grayson wasn't too confident. "I don't know."

"Sure we can. We're lots better than we were at first."

Grayson didn't know how his friend could stay so optimistic. He didn't think that he'd feel very cheerful if he had a twisted foot. "Have they collected enough money for your operation, yet?"

"Dad says they're getting close. I'd sure like to get it fixed before Christmas. It'd be the best present I ever had."

"Grayson thought that a Skylander Giant set would be the best present he ever had, but his foot was straight and he could run fast.

The summer passed, but there was no news from the sheriff's office. Grayson knew that he wouldn't have a garage to play in this winter. But when the letter came from his dad's collector friend, he forgot about scooters, wiffle balls, and Frisbees. "Dad, what does it say?"

"I'll read it." He clipped the end of the envelope and fished out the letter.

"Dear Chris,

I'm sorry to have taken so long, but I wanted to do some research before I made an offer. You have some valuable old containers here, especially the Manhattan bottle. I'll pay you one thousand dollars for the whole batch. I think that's a fair wholesale price. I might get fifteen hundred or more at auction, but I'd have to pay thirty percent commission, and you never know what they'll sell for. But I don't plan to sell. If we can agree on this price, I'll keep them for my collection.

Think it over and get back to me.

Sincerely,
Gregory Payne"

"What do you think, son?"

"A thousand dollars? That's more than enough to buy the whole Skylander Giant set."

"Mr. Ehlert told me that's the amount they need to go ahead with Alex's operation."

Grayson looked at his dad. "I should give this money to Alex?" He hadn't thought about giving his money away. Then he wouldn't get his garage or his Skylanders.

"It'll be your money, Grayson. It's your decision."

Alex was his best friend. But he wanted those Skylanders. Grayson worried about it all week. He finally decided.

After dinner that night, he told his dad, "A thousand dollars is a lot of money. Enough that I can help Alex and buy my Skylander Giant set, too. I'll give half of it to Alex. The Lion's Club can find the rest. It should be easy for them."

"That's generous, son. I'm proud of you, but—"

Grayson squirmed when his father hesitated.

"They'll get the money, but it'll probably delay Alex's operation until next spring or summer."

"I'll give him five hundred dollars. That's a lot of money."

"Yes, it is. And it's a lot of money for the Lion's Club to raise in this small community."

Grayson thought that giving five hundred dollars was very generous. He wasn't sure, but he doubted that anyone else had given that much money. He was disappointed that his dad didn't seem excited, too. But he didn't want to think about it anymore. He had told Alex that he'd meet him at the park to warm up before his father took them to the ball diamond for the last game this season.

"Dad, I'm going to the park to practice with Alex. You can pick us up there. Okay?"

Grayson was in no hurry to face Alex. At first, when he'd decided to donate five hundred dollars, he was excited. But having the operation now would sure be a nice Christmas present for his friend.

Will Alex Live?

The boys tossed the ball back and forth for a while before they began to throw hard. Mr. Meyer had told them it was important to warm up by throwing easy. That to throw hard too soon could hurt their arms. And Mr. Meyer would know. He'd coached the best team that Winneconne ever had. Grayson wasn't sure why he'd agreed to help the Butte des Morts Lion's team. He supposed that Mr. Meyer just liked baseball.

They slowly increased their distance as they threw balls back and forth. Grayson backed toward the swings, Alex toward the road. Grayson played left field and Alex played right field, so, after ten minutes of easy throwing, they began to toss high pop-ups back and forth. Grayson's dad had been working with him, so he didn't miss many balls anymore. When he could get to the ball, Alex never missed.

"Get farther back," Grayson hollered. "I'll throw one as high and far as I can."

He wound up and heaved the ball as hard as he could.

Alex turned, stumbled, righted himself, and ran toward the road, his eyes looking up toward the ball.

Grayson saw the car coming down Washington Street, but Alex didn't.

Grayson shouted, but Alex didn't stop. He continued to run and didn't slow until he heard the squeal of the brakes. When he tried to stop, he stumbled and slammed into the side of the slowing car.

Grayson was already running toward them when Alex and the car collided. When he saw his friend lying bloody and still on the pavement, he knelt by his side and grabbed his hand, but he knew better than to move him. "Alex, I'm sorry." He'd thrown the ball too far. "Are you okay?"

Alex didn't answer.

Lights flashing and siren screaming, the ambulance drove away.

Grayson's mother and father comforted him, but he felt terrible. It was his fault. "Will Alex be okay? Can we go see him?"

"Not right away, son," his father said. "I'll keep in touch with his father, and we'll go as soon as the doctors say it's okay."

Grayson didn't want to ask if he'd live. He didn't want to think about it. Alex was his best friend.

Grayson asked again that day and the next morning, too, but there was no news. He took out his Skylanders, but after setting Spyro in the portal of power, he sat and stared at the television screen. He didn't even remove Spyro from the portal before leaving the house. This time, his mother didn't complain.

Grayson walked slowly up Ontario Street toward Maple Street. All he could think about was Alex. If his twisted foot had been fixed, maybe he'd not have stumbled into that car. Or, if he hadn't thrown the ball too far? He wished that Alex was with him now, wished it had never happened.

Grayson was sitting on the swing seat when his father came running up Washington Street toward the park. Grayson saw him coming and knew there must be news. Was Alex still alive?

His father bent over to catch his wind. "Grayson," he took a deep breath, "we can go to the hospital. Alex is awake."

Grayson wanted to cry. "Will he live?"

"He'll be fine. He had a concussion and lots of cuts and bruises, but he'll be home in a couple days."

They walked down the long hallway to Alex's hospital room. Grayson knew what he must do. When he told Alex that he'd get one thousand dollars for the bottles, Alex was excited. "You'll have enough to buy that Skylander Giant set you've wanted. Will you teach me how to play?"

"No."

Alex looked disappointed. "You won't play it with me?"

"Not anytime soon. I'm not going to buy the Skylander Giant set with the money."

"You're not going to buy the set? Why?"

"I've got better plans for that money."

"There's not enough to buy a garage."

Grayson laughed but Alex looked puzzled. "Dad says that Mr. Ehlert told him they need a thousand dollars to start your operation. I'm going to donate my money to the Lion's Club. All of it."

"To fix my foot?"

And later, when the doctors said they'd do the surgery before Christmas, Alex exclaimed, "That's the best Christmas present I could ever have. Thank you, Grayson."

When Grayson handed the check to Mr. Ehlert, he knew he'd done the right thing, and it felt good. His friend would be able to run like all the rest of his baseball teammates. Grayson hoped that Santa Claus was watching.

Another Championship Game

Winter passed and, in the spring, a new baseball season began. Grayson and Alex were hopeful about their chances. "I think we can win the championship this year," Grayson said.

"I hope my foot is healed in time for me to start the season."

"Mr. Meyer says we'll be a good team if our young players have gotten better over the winter."

"I sure hope I can run faster this year."

Grayson was surprised that Alex wasn't as cheerful and confident as he'd always been.

When he told his mother, she said, "Now that Alex's foot is okay, he's probably worried that he still can't run fast."

Grayson tried to convince Alex that it would be okay, that he'd be able to run like the other boys.

But Alex's foot healed slowly, and he sat on the bench during most of the summer. That worried Alex, and it worried Grayson, too. He wanted his friend to be happy again. Maybe he shouldn't have donated that money.

But as the summer progressed, the boys had much to be happy about. Their team was competing for the championship, and Alex's spirits seemed to perk up as he sat cheering for his teammates during each of their wins.

And Grayson thought that Alex was running better, too.

At the end of the summer, two teams were tied for first place, the Butte des Morts Lions and Winneconne Wolves. They had already played twice that summer, each team winning one, and this last game would be the tie-breaker.

Before the game, Mr. Meyer called his team together. "Boys, I don't need to tell you to try your best. You've done that all summer and I know you will now. Whether we win or lose, I'm proud of you." He raised his hand and called, "High—" but he lowered it and said, "One more thing. I'm starting Alex in right field today." He raised his hand again and called, "High five, everyone. Now go out there and win this game."

Grayson was surprised but happy for his friend.

Alex didn't say anything, but Grayson was glad to see him smile as he reached under the bench for his glove.

Not everyone was happy about Alex playing again. Some of the boys complained. Grayson heard, "This game's too important to let him play. We could have won two years ago, but he lost it for us."

Grayson hoped Alex would do well, that he wouldn't be responsible for the game's outcome.

The score was tied in the last inning, with the Lions having last-ups. If they scored, they'd win.

But the first two batters made outs, so it didn't look very promising. And Alex would be responsible for the outcome. Grayson was on-deck, watching Alex take his practice swings. Grayson hoped that his friend could get on base so that he'd have a chance to bat. But neither boy had a base hit all day, and although Alex had hit the ball hard, Grayson had struck out twice and popped out his third at bat. It just wasn't his day. He hoped that he was due to get a hit. But, first, his friend would have to get on base somehow.

Alex swung at a bad pitch and missed.

"Come on, Alex," Grayson called, "just swing at strikes." He hoped that his friend could get a walk or get on base with an error.

Grayson began to concentrate on his turn at bat. Coach said to keep his eye on the ball, that he was pulling his head out too soon.

Alex fouled off a pitch.

Then the pitcher threw three straight balls, each one close, but Alex didn't swing.

Now Grayson worried that Alex's bat was frozen on his shoulder, that he'd take a third strike.

Three balls and two strikes. Down to the last pitch. Grayson began to think that he wouldn't get a chance. He waggled his bat.

Coach Meyer called time out and motioned to Alex. Grayson heard him say, "Just relax, Alex. I'm not going to coach next year. But I'll always remember your bravery. I'm proud of you. Go do your best, son."

And when the pitch came in, Alex hit it hard. He ran toward first, faster than Grayson had ever seen him run before. He was on his way toward a double.

Grayson stepped toward the plate. He would get to bat. He hoped he could do as well as his friend.

But Alex didn't stop running. When the ball went through the outfielder's legs, Alex was almost to third. But when he rounded third toward home, he stumbled.

Grayson turned away. He didn't want to look.

When he heard their fans cheer, he looked back and saw Alex streaking toward home, but the ball was in the pitcher's hand. The pitcher turned and threw a perfect strike to the catcher, who stood erect on home plate. The catcher scooped the ball from the air and swept it down to tag Alex as he slid into home plate.

The umpire jumped in front of the plate and swept both hands down into the safe sign.

Alex had done it. This year they won the championship.

As they walked together, arms around each other's shoulders, Grayson's dad ran up to them. "Great job, Alex." He hugged them both. "And, Grayson, I just received a letter from the preservation program. They said we can go ahead and dig. Those bones weren't human, after all. We'll have our garage before the snow falls."

This was the best day of Grayson's life. He could see that Alex was the happiest he'd been all summer—and that made the day even better.

"Let's go to my house and play Skylander Giant, Alex."

They walked arm-in-arm toward home.

He'd hardly had a chance to play Skylander Giant since he got it for Christmas. And Grayson knew that today, KAOS would go down.

Grayson's Garage:
Glossary of Sergeant Digby's British Slang

Sergeant Digby says about Harry: "He's an addled bloke, but he's cool beans, alright. Those knob heads think they'll filch his cheese, but they don't know diddly squat. One of these days Harry'll throw a wobbler and pepper their behinds. And that'll be ticketyboo with me."

What the sergeant means is: "He's a silly fellow, but he's cool, alright. Those foolish fellows think they'll steal his cheese, but they know nothing. One of these days Harry'll get very angry and shoot them in the backsides. And that'll be very good with me."

addled bloke: silly chap

adjutant: someone who assists a commanding officer

Big War: World War II

bimble: walk

bits and bobs: various things

bonkers: angry

brass tacks: the important task

brigade: a military group

British Expeditionary Force: British army stationed in France through 1940

Chap: a male

clapped out: worn out

cool beans: cool, good

daft: foolish

demolition man: handles explosives

diddly squat: knows nothing

dipstick: silly person

Harold William Thorpe

Dunkirk: French town where a battle was fought during World War II

elbow grease: lots of effort

eye up: look out

fam: family member

filch: steal

hain't: ain't

heave ho: finishing a relationship

jim jams: pajamas

kibosh: put an end to a thing

kip: short nap

knob heads: foolish fellows

knows his onions: very knowledgeable

nosebag: food

not on your Nelly: never

pepper their behinds: shoot things at their backside

prim 'n' proper: behaves in a correct way

raddle: confused

set charges: set out explosives

Tention!: attention!

that's sound: good, great

thingy: something whose name can't be recalled

throw a wobbler: get very angry

ticketyboo: very good

top banana: most important person

wad: money

whole shebang: the entire amount

About the Author

Harold William Thorpe grew up in Southwest Wisconsin, living in Mineral Point, Ridgeway, and Dodgeville before graduating from Barneveld High School. After high school, he earned an education degree from UW-Platteville. He then worked for eleven years in Janesville, Wisconsin — first as a general education and special education teacher, then the last four years as a school psychologist. During these years he started a business and earned a masters degree in educational psychology from UW-Madison. Afterward, he left Janesville for Utah State University where he earned a doctorate degree in education.

Upon returning to Wisconsin he took a position at UW-Oshkosh, where he initiated a program that prepared college students to teach children with learning disabilities. For the next twenty-five years he taught classes, supervised undergraduate and graduate student teachers, and served in administrative positions as a graduate program coordinator, a department chairperson, and a college associate dean. But his first love was conducting research that produced more than twenty-five publications in education and psychology journals. At the end of his career he headed a research project that resulted in the return of fifty-two million dollars from the Federal Department of Education to Wisconsin schools.

He lives in Butte des Morts, Wisconsin, a small lakeside community near Oshkosh. Although he had published non-fiction books, upon retirement he decided to learn how to write fiction. He recently published *Giddyap Tin Lizzie*, *Bittersweet Harvest*, and his first children's chapter book, *Wyatt's Woods*, which is set in the woods surrounding his home in Door County, Wisconsin. He followed *Wyatt's Woods* with *Aubrey's Attic*, set in the historic community of Butte des Morts and Winneconne, the neighboring community where his granddaughter Aubrey attends school. *Grayson's Garage* is also set in Butte des Morts. *Bellamy's Ball*, a picture book, will be published soon.